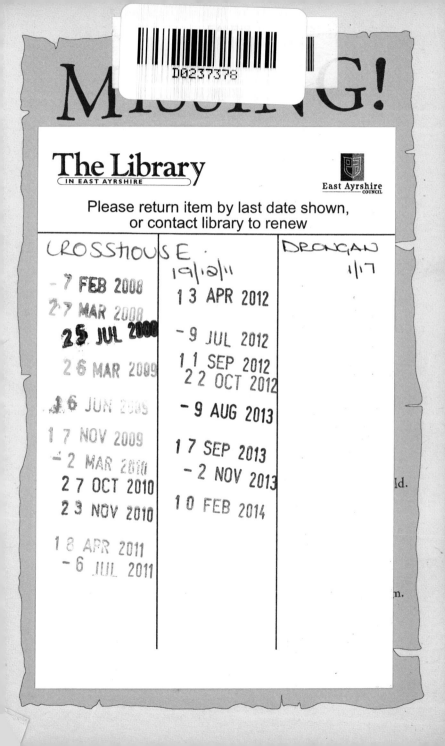

Sue Bentley's books for children often include animals or fairies. She lives in Northampton and enjoys reading, going to the cinema, and sitting watching the frogs and newts in her garden pond. If she hadn't been a writer she would probably have been a skydiver or brain surgeon. The main reason she writes is that she can drink pots and pots of tea while she's typing. She has met and owned many cats and each one has brought a special sort of magic to her life.

Magic Kitten

A Shimmering Splash

SUE BENTLEY

Illustrated by Angela Swan

PUFFIN

To Biff, the toothless tabby with issues

PUFFIN BOOKS

Published by the Penguin Group
Penguin Books Ltd, 80 Strand, London WC2R ORL, England
Penguin Group (USA) Inc., 375 Hudson Street, New York, New York 10014, USA
Penguin Group (Canada), 90 Eglinton Avenue East, Suite 700, Toronto, Ontario, Canada M4P 2Y3
(a division of Pearson Penguin Canada Inc.)
Penguin Ireland, 25 St Stephen's Green, Dublin 2, Ireland (a division of Penguin Books Ltd)
Penguin Group (Australia), 250 Camberwell Road, Camberwell, Victoria 3124, Australia
(a division of Pearson Australia Group Pty Ltd)
Penguin Books India Pvt Ltd, 11 Community Centre, Panchsheel Park,
New Delhi – 110 017, India
Penguin Group (NZ), 67 Apollo Drive, Rosedale, North Shore 0632, New Zealand
(a division of Pearson New Zealand Ltd)
Penguin Books (South Africa) (Pty) Ltd, 24 Sturdee Avenue, Rosebank,
Johannesburg 2196, South Africa

Penguin Books Ltd, Registered Offices: 80 Strand, London WC2R ORL, England

puffinbooks.com

First published 2007
1

Text copyright © Susan Bentley, 2007
Illustrations copyright © Angela Swan, 2007
All rights reserved

The moral right of the author and illustrator has been asserted

Set in Bembo
Typeset by Palimpsest Book Production Limited, Grangemouth, Stirlingshire
Made and printed in England by Clays Ltd, St Ives plc

British Library Cataloguing in Publication Data
A CIP catalogue record for this book is available from the British Library

ISBN: 978-0-141-32200-1

Prologue

The young white lion dipped his head towards the pool and drank deeply. It felt good to taste the water of his home again. Perhaps this time it would be safe to stay.

Suddenly, across the pool, a huge black adult lion emerged from some trees and leapt up on to the rocks.

'Ebony!' Flame gasped, as he looked

up at the terrifying sight of his
uncle.

He felt sparks crackling in his fur and
there was a bright white flash. Where
the majestic young white lion had
stood now crouched a tiny fluffy amber
and white kitten with a big amber
patch over one eye.

Flame's furry kitten tummy brushed
the ground as he edged slowly
backwards into the shelter of some
tall rushes. As he lay there trembling
with fear, hoping desperately that he
had hidden in time, the rushes parted
and a large dark shape came towards
him.

Flame's tiny heart missed a beat. This
was it! Ebony had found him!

'Prince Flame,' rumbled a deep gentle

voice. 'I am glad to see you, but it is not yet safe for you to return.'

Flame blinked at the adult grey lion in relief. 'Cirrus. It is good to see you again. Tell me, how is my uncle ruling the kingdom he stole from me?'

Cirrus showed worn teeth as his lip curled with anger. 'Ebony is strong and cruel and will never change. He is determined to find you and kill you so that he can rule forever.'

'I am ready to face him now and take back my throne!' Flame mewed, his emerald eyes flashing with anger.

Cirrus nodded approvingly and reached out an enormous grey paw to draw the tiny kitten closer. 'Bravely said, but you must first grow strong and wise. Use this disguise and go back to hide in the other world where you will be safe.'

'Nowhere is safe from my uncle's spies!' Flame answered.

As if in reply, another terrifying roar rang out. 'I sense my nephew! Where are you, Flame? Show yourself!' growled an icy voice.

'Ebony knows you're close. Go now, Flame,' Cirrus urged. 'Save yourself!'

The tiny amber and white kitten whined as he felt the power building inside him. His fluffy fur ignited with sparks and there was another bright flash.

Flame felt himself falling. Falling . . .

Chapter
ONE

Lorna Edwards caught her breath with
excitement as the car drove off the
ferry. In front of her there was a wild
landscape of mountains, lakes and vast
open spaces. Fluffy white clouds floated
in the clear blue sky.

'Craggen is so gorgeous. I really love
being back here!' she exclaimed.

'Me too,' Flora Edwards said, turning

her head to smile at her daughter.
'I expect you're dying to catch up with
Ruth and Callum.'

Lorna nodded. 'I can't wait.' It had
been almost a year since she'd seen her
cousins, who lived on the island off the
north coast of Scotland. Now she was
going to spend the whole of the school
holidays with them.

'You won't have to wait long. Marie and Hugh and the kids always come to meet us,' Lorna's mum reminded her.

Lorna leaned forward, pushing back a strand of her short red hair as she peered out at the single-track road. Just inland, the moors were dotted with huge grey stones and patches of yellow gorse. Lorna suddenly caught sight of some familiar figures, standing next to a parked car. 'There they are!' she cried, bouncing up and down in her seat with excitement.

She could see Aunt Marie, Uncle Hugh and Ruth, but Callum didn't seem to be with them. The minute their car stopped, Lorna opened the door and flew across to her aunt and uncle and cousin. Everyone began speaking at once and it was hugs all round.

'Lorna! Och, you've grown tall since last we saw you,' Uncle Hugh boomed. He was tall, with broad shoulders and dark hair and he towered over his tiny wife.

'So you have,' Aunt Marie agreed in her soft voice, pushing back a strand of curly red hair. 'I expect you'll notice the difference in Ruth too.'

'Hi!' Lorna grinned at Ruth and gave her cousin a hug. At nine years old, Ruth was a year younger than Lorna. She had dark hair, like her dad and her mum's sunny smile.

'Why do adults always go on about how much you've grown?' Ruth whispered, pulling a face.

'I know,' Lorna said, giggling. 'What do they expect us to do, shrink or something?' She glanced round at the car, expecting the back door to open at any minute. It was just like Callum to hide inside and then jump out! But the car was empty. 'OK, I give up! Where's Callum hiding?' she said, grinning.

Ruth's face seemed to cloud over. 'He didn't come. He went to a friend's house to do some homework. He said he'd see you at the farmhouse later.'

'Oh,' Lorna said, trying hard not to feel disappointed that her favourite cousin had chosen to do something else instead of coming to meet her.

'Shall we go?' Aunt Marie suggested. 'I expect you'd like to relax over a cup of tea and a bite to eat after your long journey.'

'Can I go in Aunt Marie's car?' Lorna asked her parents.

'Course you can, love. I expect you and Ruth have a lot of catching up to do,' her dad replied.

'Here now, let me give you both a hand!' Uncle Hugh said, with a gleam in his eye.

'Uh-oh!' Remembering her uncle's cheeky sense of humour, Lorna attempted to dart out of his reach, but she was too late. Hugh swept her up and tucked her under one arm and then did the same to Ruth. Marching over to the car, he piled them both into the back seat, where they collapsed together, laughing breathlessly.

Lorna's parents laughed too. Aunt Marie shook her head. 'Och! I don't think Hugh will ever grow up!' she said with a fond sigh.

Lorna linked arms with Ruth in the back, as they drove towards the farmhouse. It was good to be back on Craggen, but it did feel strange not having Callum there too.

'Thanks, Aunt Marie. That was yummy,' Lorna said, as she finished the last mouthful of delicious home-made cake. She and Ruth were sitting on the battered sofa in the comfy farmhouse kitchen.

Lorna's parents and her aunt and uncle were seated at the table. 'Why don't you show Lorna my smart new

workroom, Ruth?' Aunt Marie
suggested as she passed her husband a
second huge slice of cake.

'Do you want to see it?' Ruth asked,
looking across at Lorna.

'OK,' Lorna said. It had to be better
than listening to the grown-ups
gossiping. She followed her cousin
outside and they went across the yard
to some stone outbuildings.

'This is it,' Ruth said.

'It's um . . . very nice,' Lorna said, being polite. She peeped through the workroom window. She could see the big loom her aunt used to weave blankets and throws from their own sheep. Colourful balls of the wool, which she dyed herself, were heaped in baskets.

Ruth dug her in the ribs. 'Yeah, but weaving and stuff's dead boring. Why don't you come and see Mum's new sheep?'

Lorna grinned. This was more like it! She loved animals and her aunt and uncle kept all kinds of unusual sheep.

Ruth stopped beside a pen and pointed at six small sheep with dainty black and white faces under crinkly woollen fringes.

'Wow! They're lovely,' Lorna said. 'What sort are they?'

Before Ruth could answer, a moody voice cut in. 'Who cares? They're just stupid sheep!'

'Callum!' Lorna felt a big grin stretching across her face as she turned round. 'You're back!'

'Looks like it, doesn't it?' Callum muttered. He had his hands thrust into his jeans' pockets and his dark hair flopped forward on to his forehead.

Lorna's smile wavered a bit. 'It's really great to be here for two whole weeks,' she said anyway, hoping to encourage Callum to be a bit more friendly.

'Whatever!' He shrugged. 'I'm going inside. I'm hungry.'

'OK. See you . . . er . . . later then,'
Lorna stammered.

Callum didn't answer. Hunching his
shoulders, he crossed the yard and
disappeared into the farmhouse.

Lorna stared after him, feeling puzzled
and hurt. 'What's wrong with him?' she
asked Ruth.

'You know what boys are like,' Ruth said, rolling her eyes. 'You can't say anything to them without getting your head bitten off.'

'Most boys. But Callum's not usually like –' Lorna began.

'Stop going on about him, will you?' Ruth broke in and then she bit her lip. 'Sorry. I . . . I didn't mean to snap.'

'That's OK,' Lorna said quietly.

'I think I'll go up to my room. Mum's made up the spare bed for you in there. Are you coming?' Ruth asked.

'I'll come in a minute,' Lorna said, still feeling a bit confused. Both of her cousins were acting really weird. She waited until Ruth went inside and then sighed as she started after her.

As she trudged past the outbuildings,

a flash of bright light suddenly lit up the workshop windows. Lorna stopped, shocked. *Strange*, she thought, *I'm sure the workshop was empty*. She reached out to give the door a push. 'Hello? Is someone there?'

As the door swung open, revealing the darkened room, Lorna saw the outline of what looked to be a tiny toy kitten sitting on a basket of wool. In the dimness, it glowed as if its fur and

whiskers were dotted with a thousand tiny sparkling diamonds.

The fluffy toy must be her aunt's lucky mascot. Lorna wondered how she had missed seeing it earlier. 'Aren't you gorgeous? You look as if you're really alive,' she exclaimed.

The kitten looked up at Lorna with bright green eyes that shone in the dark. 'I am alive. Please can you help me?' it mewed.

Chapter
★TWO★

Lorna gasped with shock as she
fumbled for the light switch. She could
have sworn that the toy kitten had just
spoken to her!

In the dim light, Lorna could see
that the kitten had fluffy amber and
white fur, with an amber patch over
one eye, a bright pink nose and the
biggest emerald eyes she had ever seen.

It did look very realistic. She moved forward for a closer look. But just as she did the kitten raised its tiny head.

'I am Prince Flame, heir to the Lion Throne. Who are you?' it miaowed inquisitively.

'You really did just speak!' Lorna spluttered. 'I'm . . . um, Lorna Edwards. I'm . . . staying here on Craggen Island with my cousins for the school holidays.' She was finding it difficult to

take this in. Talking animals only existed in fairy stories – they didn't just turn up in real life! Bending down, she tried to make herself seem smaller, so the amazing kitten wouldn't run away.

'Did you say you're a prince?' she asked him.

Flame nodded, his green eyes gleaming with anger. 'But my Uncle Ebony has stolen my throne and rules in my place. One day I will return to challenge him and regain my throne!'

'You're a bit small for that. If I were you, I'd wait until I'd grown up,' Lorna advised gently.

Flame didn't reply, but instead Lorna saw silver sparks beginning to glitter in Flame's fluffy fur. He sprang off the basket of wool and before Lorna could move, she was blinded by another bright silver flash that filled the room.

'Oh!' Lorna rubbed her eyes. When she looked again she saw that the tiny kitten had disappeared and in its place stood a magnificent young pure-white lion.

Lorna caught her breath, eyeing the huge paws and sharp teeth. 'Flame?'

'Do not be afraid. I will not harm you,' the lion told her in a deep velvety roar. There was a final dazzling flash of light and Flame magically reappeared before her as a tiny amber and white kitten, with an amber patch over one eye.

'Wow! That's a brilliant disguise. No one would guess that you're a Lion Prince!' Lorna exclaimed.

'I must hide from my uncle's spies

now. Can you help me, Lorna?' the tiny kitten mewed, trembling from head to toe.

'Of course I will!' Lorna said, picking him up. Flame was impressive as his real lion self, but in his helpless kitten disguise he was just adorable. 'Come on. Let's go into the farmhouse. You're going to love meeting all the family.'

'No!' Flame twisted round and gazed up at her. 'You can tell no one that I am a prince. It must be our secret!'

Lorna felt a bit disappointed that she couldn't even tell Ruth about Flame but she sighed as she thought sadly that both her cousins didn't seem that delighted to see her anyway. Lorna felt determined to do whatever Flame wanted to keep him safe. 'OK. Don't worry, I won't give anything away. I'll just say you're a stray or something.'

Flame relaxed and blinked up at her with narrowed trusting eyes. 'Thank you, Lorna.'

'That's all right. Let's go and find you something to eat. I bet you're hungry,' she said.

Flame purred eagerly.

As Lorna crossed the yard, she smiled. Her holiday had just taken an amazingly unexpected turn!

'What a cute little kitten – and I really like his name,' Aunt Marie said, when Lorna had finished introducing Flame. 'He must have smelt the farm cats and come looking for food. We've had a few other strays turn up out of the blue.'

'Yes, that's what must have happened,'
Lorna said, glad that she didn't have to
go into more detail about finding
Flame. 'I promised him . . . um, I mean,
I promised myself . . .' she corrected
quickly, '. . . that I'd look after him. Is it
OK if I keep him?' she asked in her
best pleading voice.

'Now, Lorna . . .' her mum said
warningly.

Uncle Hugh laughed. 'It's fine by us,

isn't it, Marie?' he said, turning towards his wife. 'Och! One more cat won't make much difference and I don't expect this wee chap will eat much!'

'Only if you're sure . . .' Lorna's mum said, looking at Marie.

Aunt Marie smiled in agreement. 'There's cat food in the barn and some old blankets you can use for Flame's bed.'

'Thanks!' Lorna beamed at her aunt and uncle. 'I'll feed Flame and then make him a bed in Ruth's room. Come on, Flame!' she called, going outside quickly before anyone could object. There was no way she was going to let her tiny new friend sleep in a draughty old barn!

★

Lorna slept well and woke to find bright sunlight pushing through a pair of unfamiliar blue curtains. It was a moment before she remembered that she was in the spare bed in Ruth's bedroom with Flame's tiny warm body curled up beside her.

'Hello, you,' she whispered, stroking his soft ears. 'Did you sleep well?'

'Yes, thank you. I feel safe here with you,' Flame purred softly.

Ruth's bed was empty and Lorna assumed that her cousin had already gone downstairs. She jumped out of bed. 'Let's go and get some breakfast,' she said to Flame.

Halfway down the stairs, with Flame at her heels, Lorna heard raised voices. She paused and Flame stopped beside her.

'Aw, do I have to come too, Dad?'
Callum was complaining. 'It's dead
boring. Anyway, I've made plans to
meet my friends.'

'I'm afraid you'll have to meet them
later,' Hugh replied firmly. 'You knew
I'd need your help. Besides, I'd have
thought you'd want to spend some time
with Lorna. You've hardly said two
words to her since she arrived.'

'OK then, if I have to,' Callum
grumbled.

Lorna heard the bathroom door close and then Ruth came down the stairs behind her. 'What are you waiting here for?' she asked.

'Nothing,' Lorna said quickly, feeling a bit guilty for eavesdropping.

She, Flame and Ruth went into the kitchen. Callum was sitting with his chin propped on his hand, slowly stirring a spoon around in a bowl of porridge.

'Hi, Callum,' Lorna said.

Callum grunted a reply.

'Hello, girls. Help yourselves to porridge,' Hugh said cheerfully, waving his spoon towards the steaming pot on the stove. 'Eat up. We'll have to get cracking soon.'

'Where are we going, Uncle Hugh?'

Lorna asked as she fed Flame, before spooning creamy porridge into a bowl.

'We're driving to one of the coves. I have to do a beach clean-up and litter survey,' Hugh replied.

'Dad's just been made a part-time warden for the nature reserve,' Ruth said proudly.

'Big deal,' Callum said under his breath.

Hugh grinned patiently. 'Cheer up, lad! I know picking up litter's not very exciting, but with a bit of luck we'll see some seals with their pups.'

'Seal pups? Wow!' Lorna didn't care if she had to pick up litter all day, if it meant she got to see some seals. She couldn't wait to see what Flame would make of them.

Chapter
THREE

'Bye! See you later!' Lorna called to her parents and her aunt, who were staying behind at the farm. She picked Flame up before getting into Hugh's Land Rover.

Flame sat on Lorna's lap for the short drive to the cove. Lorna stroked his soft ears, as he peered out at the cliffs and the sun sparkling on the blue sea.

Once they were all standing on the
white sand of the little cove, Hugh
doled out black plastic sacks and
protective gloves. 'Just chuck any litter
inside. Cans, plastic bags, bits of old
beach ball, whatever. Then we'll list
everything you've collected when we
meet back here in an hour or so,' he
instructed.

'OK, Dad,' Ruth said. 'Come on,
Lorna. Let's do our collecting together.'

As Lorna and Ruth headed towards the shore, Hugh and Callum went off towards the cliffs. Lorna could see that her cousin's shoulders were hunched and he was dragging his feet. 'Looks like Callum would rather be ten million miles away!' she said, frowning.

Ruth glared at her brother. 'Or fishing with his new *best* friends!' She stamped on a discarded paper cup until it was as flat as a pancake and then stuffed it into her sack. Turning her back, she moved away up the beach and began picking up litter.

Lorna stared after her, blinking in surprise. 'I thought we were supposed to be doing this together,' she whispered to Flame. 'Ruth's as bad as Callum!

One minute she's all friendly and then she's in a major stressy! I don't get it.'

Flame's furry brow crinkled in a frown. 'Perhaps you could ask her what is wrong when she is in a better mood.'

Lorna nodded. 'Good idea, Flame. I'll do that. Come on, let's collect litter.'

The tiny kitten pawed at shells and pebbles, scooting sideways and play-growling. Lorna laughed at his antics and soon forgot about her two unpredictable cousins. As she gradually filled the sack, Lorna found that she'd moved closer to a big cluster of rocks at the shore.

One of the small greyish rocks was half submerged by the sea. But to Lorna's surprise it suddenly moved. It wasn't a rock. It was a baby seal!

'Look over here, Flame!' she
whispered, slowly moving closer. Flame
padded after her, his ears pricked
expectantly.

'Oh, no,' Lorna gasped in dismay, as
she spotted the tough fishing line
which was tangled round the seal pup's
flippers and tail. 'The poor little thing.
It looks exhausted. I bet it's been trying
to get free for ages.'

Flame gave a mew of sympathy.

The pup struggled weakly, looking up
at her with big helpless dark eyes. Its
head drooped and it flopped back down
on to the wet sand.

'Don't worry. I'm going to help you,'
Lorna crooned. She went right up to
the pup, bent down, and began gently
trying to untangle the fishing line.

Then from out of the corner of her
eye she caught a sudden movement as
an enormous seal appeared from behind
the rocks. Baring its strong teeth and
barking with rage, it came towards
Lorna.

The mother seal! It thought Lorna
was trying to hurt its baby.

'It's OK. I'm just . . . just trying to
help,' Lorna gulped, edging backwards.
Her foot struck a small half-buried
rock and she fell backwards on to the
damp sand.

The mother seal rolled her dark eyes
and hissed with fury. As she lunged
forward, ready to attack, Lorna bit back
a scream.

Time seemed to stand still. But then a
warm tingle flowed down Lorna's spine.

Huge silver sparks began to glow again in Flame's soft fur. The kitten lifted a tiny amber, white-tipped paw and a bright stream of sparks shot out from it, raining down gently on the enraged mother seal and her baby.

The mother seal stopped dead abruptly and seemed to calm down. Lorna looked on in surprise as, with a loud whipping noise, the tangled fishing line instantly began to unravel all by

itself. In a few seconds, the pup's
flippers and tail were free and the
fishing line lay on the sand in a tangled
heap. The pup shook itself and then
began slithering towards the sea.

The mother seal took a last long look
at Lorna and then followed her baby.

Lorna got up, her heart still beating
fast. She brushed wet sand from her

jeans as she watched the seals move into deeper water and then swim away together. She was pleased they were both OK, even though she still felt quite shocked by what had just happened.

She turned to Flame. 'Phew! Thanks for saving me! That was *way* too close.'

'You are welcome,' Flame mewed.

Just as the very last spark faded from Flame's amber and white fur, Hugh, Callum and Ruth came dashing round the rocks. 'Are you all right?' Uncle Hugh cried, white-faced. 'I heard a seal's distress cry then saw a mother and her pup swimming away! What happened?'

'I'm fine.' Lorna told her uncle about finding the baby seal, but played down the part about the mother seal. 'I . . . um, managed to untangle the fishing line and pull it off,' she fibbed.

Hugh frowned. 'Thank goodness for that! You seem to have done a brilliant job, but don't ever, ever try anything like that by yourself again. You should have called to me for help. Mother seals can be very dangerous when they're protecting their young! She could have attacked you.'

Tell me about it, Lorna thought; her heartbeat had only just about returned to normal.

Ruth looked at Lorna admiringly. 'Crikey! You were brave.'

'Not really. I was scared to death!' Lorna admitted.

Even Callum looked impressed. 'Way

to go, Lorna,' he said, giving her a big grin.

Lorna grinned back. It was the first time since she'd arrived that Callum seemed like his old self.

Hugh picked up the broken fishing line. 'I wish the idiots who leave this stuff around could see what harm it causes. Most fishermen are responsible types, but the few who aren't spoil it for the others . . .'

'Do you need me any more, Dad?' Callum broke in impatiently. 'Only I'm supposed to be meeting my friends, remember?'

'What?' Hugh looked at his son. 'All right. I suppose I can manage without you now. Where are you going?'

'Just to a classmate's house. See you

later, everyone!' Callum called, already jogging towards a track that led inland from the beach.

'Callum!' Ruth called after her brother, but he didn't turn round. Only Lorna saw the worried look on Ruth's face, which she quickly changed to a smile as she turned back towards her dad.

Chapter
FOUR

Lorna and Ruth finished helping Hugh list all the beach litter for the survey. It seemed to take ages and Lorna was glad when they were finally putting the bags of litter, clipboards and pens into her uncle's car.

'Thanks very much, girls – and kitten,' Hugh said, bending down to stroke Flame's fluffy amber and white fur.

'I think you all deserve a treat after your hard work. How does hot chocolate with extra whipped cream sound? Come on. We'll go to the cafe in the high street!'

'Yes!' Lorna and Ruth chorused.

Flame gave an eager mew.

Hugh laughed. 'Sounds like Flame's looking forward to a saucer of cream!

I reckon that wee kitten understands everything we say.'

Lorna smiled to herself. If only Uncle Hugh knew!

It was a short drive to the high street shops. On the way Hugh discovered a grocery list in his pocket. 'Och! I've just remembered that I promised to bring some things back for Marie. I just need to nip into the supermarket.' He pulled into the car park and parked the car. 'This won't take long. You may as well wait in the car and then we'll go straight to the cafe.'

'OK, Dad,' Ruth said.

Lorna sat in the back of the Land Rover with Flame on her lap as Hugh disappeared into the supermarket. She glanced around idly and noticed some

boys messing about near a trolley
park. One of them looked familiar.
'That looks like Callum over there,'
she said.

'Where?' Ruth turned her head. 'It *is*
him! I knew he wasn't going to one of
his classmates'. He's with those older
boys again. The one with the black hair
is called Sam and the one with a round
face and freckles is Laurie.'

'You don't seem to like them very
much,' Lorna said.

'I don't!' Ruth said. 'Sam and Laurie
are always getting into trouble. Mum
and Dad don't know that Callum hangs
about with them.'

Things started to fall into place for
Lorna. 'But you knew, didn't you?'

Ruth nodded unhappily. 'I found out

when I saw Callum with them in the
park.'

'Maybe you should tell your mum
and dad what's going on,' Lorna
suggested.

'I'm not a snitch!' Ruth said
indignantly, glancing over at the three
boys again. 'But if Dad sees them
together he'll go bananas. I've got to
warn Callum to stay out of sight.' She
got out of the car and started hurrying
over to the trolley park.

'Come on, Flame. Let's follow her!'
Lorna said, setting Flame down on the
ground. As she strode after Ruth, he
scampered along at her heels. Lorna saw
Sam climbing into a trolley and then
Callum and Laurie began dragging it
around in circles.

'Hey!' Ruth called. As she almost reached the boys, they gave the trolley an extra big shove and let it go.

It zoomed past Ruth and hurtled straight at Lorna and Flame. Lorna quickly stepped sideways, but Flame's tiny legs couldn't move fast enough. The heavy trolley veered towards him, wheels rattling. He was about to be run over!

'Flame! Look out!' Lorna cried. She knew he couldn't use his magic without giving himself away.

Throwing herself forward, she reached desperately for the trolley. Her fingers brushed against the metal side and then just managed to grab hold of it. The trolley swung sideways, wrenching her arm painfully and missing Flame by a whisker, before it trundled away across the car park.

'Ow!' Lorna cried out as a hot wave of pain shot up her arm.

But Flame was safe. He bounded up to her and twined himself round her ankles. 'Thank you, Lorna,' he purred softly. 'But I am sorry that you were hurt when you were saving me.'

'I'll be OK,' Lorna whispered bravely, although she could almost feel the

colour draining out of her face. 'I'd hate it if anything happened to you.'

The trolley had stopped now and Sam climbed out. 'What did you grab it for? It almost tipped over!' he shouted at Lorna.

Callum came running over with Laurie at his side. 'What are you doing here anyway? Are you spying on me, you rotten little sneak?' Callum hissed at Ruth.

Despite her sore arm, Lorna felt her temper rising. 'Oh shut up, Callum! Ruth didn't even know you were here! Uncle Hugh just called in for some shopping. But you and your stupid friends just nearly ran Flame over!' she stormed.

Sam's eyes narrowed and he took a

step towards Lorna. 'What did you just call us?'

'It's OK, Sam. She's my cousin,' Callum said hastily. He turned to Lorna. 'You shouldn't have interfered. It's your fault if that kitten got in the way!'

'For goodness' sake, Callum! Can't you see that Lorna's hurt her arm?' Ruth shouted, almost in tears.

Callum's face straightened. 'I didn't realize. Sorry, Lorna. Is it bad?'

Sam and Laurie exchanged sly looks. 'Gotta go!' Sam said.

'Me too! Let's leg it!' Laurie said.

'Typical!' Ruth said to Callum as both boys ran away. 'I don't think much of your precious friends!' She turned to Lorna. 'Let's go and find Dad. He'll know what to do.'

Lorna's arm was aching so much now
that she didn't argue. She scooped
Flame up with her good arm and held
him against her side as she followed
Ruth.

Callum stood there, undecided.
'There's no point me coming with you.
I can't do anything. What are you going
to tell Dad?'

'I don't know yet,' Ruth called back.

'Hadn't you better go after Sam and Laurie before he sees you?'

'Ruth . . .' Callum began, but then he stopped and his face took on the grumpy expression that Lorna was getting used to seeing. 'I hope your arm's OK,' Callum said quickly to her, before turning and going after his friends.

'If you can find somewhere where we can be alone, I will make your arm better,' Flame purred softly to Lorna.

Lorna nodded, wincing. As they went inside the supermarket, she spotted the ladies' loos. 'I'm just going to pop in here,' she said to Ruth.

'Shall I come in with you?' Ruth asked.

Lorna shook her head. 'No. I'll be fine.'

'All right. I'll wait outside,' Ruth said.

Luckily there was no one else in the toilets. As Lorna closed the door, big silver sparks were already igniting in Flame's amber and white fur and his whiskers crackled with electricity. He lifted a tiny paw and sent a spray of twinkling glitter towards Lorna's sore

arm. It showered gently on to her and immediately her arm felt all warm and tingly. The pain increased for a second and then it seemed to drain down her arm and flow right out of the ends of her fingers.

'Wow! Thanks, Flame. My arm feels fine now,' she said. She gave him an affectionate cuddle and he licked her chin with his rough little tongue. A few seconds later she emerged from the loo carrying Flame in both arms.

Ruth gave her a puzzled look. 'Your arm seems a lot better.'

'It's absolutely fine now. I er . . . splashed cold water on it,' Lorna said. 'Mum did that when I hit my knee once. It worked great. No need to say anything to Uncle Hugh.'

'Hello, you two. Did you get bored waiting for me?' Hugh came towards them, holding plastic bags of shopping.

'Yes, we did,' Lorna said, smiling brightly. 'Can we go to the cafe now, please?'

Chapter
FIVE

'Dad has to go across to one of the
smaller islands today. We're all going
with him and taking a picnic lunch,'
Ruth said the following day.

'Sounds great!' Lorna said. 'Is Callum
coming too?'

Ruth nodded. 'He's been on his
best behaviour since yesterday. I
reckon he's still worried that I'll tell

Dad about what happened in the car park.'

'Are you going to?' Lorna asked.

'No!' Ruth shook her head, grinning. 'But don't tell Callum!'

They both laughed.

Lorna went to fetch her shoulder bag. She put the bag on to the floor, so that Flame could jump inside before they all walked down to the small jetty, which was immediately beyond the back garden.

As Lorna climbed into *Seagull*, Hugh's small but powerful motorboat, the sea breeze ruffled her short red hair. She shaded her eyes with her hand, looking at the humped shapes of the islands across the narrow channel.

Callum stood waiting until everyone except Hugh was on board. 'Can I go across in the dinghy instead of coming with you, Dad?'

Hugh thought about it and then shook his head. 'It's not safe today. There's a chance of storms and high tides. I'd rather we all went in *Seagull*.'

'Aw, Da-ad. I've been over to the islands in the dinghy heaps of times. I'm a strong rower,' Callum grumbled.

Hugh gave him a level look. 'I'm not going to argue with you, Callum.'

Sighing heavily, Callum got on board *Seagull* and plonked himself down next to Lorna. Hugh got into the cabin and started the engine and the boat moved away from the jetty.

Flame sat on Lorna's lap, his nose in the air as he sniffed the sea breeze. The boat slapped against the waves and Lorna tasted salty spray on her lips.

In only a few minutes they were drawing level with some sandbanks. Dozens of mother seals and their pups were dotted all over them.

'I wonder if the pup we . . . er, I mean *I* untangled, is over there with its mum,' Lorna said. She felt Flame nudge her hand as she corrected herself in front of the others.

'The pups only stay with their

mothers for a couple of weeks. Then they're off to fend for themselves,' Hugh told Lorna. He slowed *Seagull*'s engine, so everyone could have a good look at the seals before then steering the boat towards the island.

Once *Seagull* was moored, everyone got out and trudged up the beach with the picnic things.

As Lorna helped spread out a tartan rug, hundreds of gulls and fulmars wheeled overhead and puffins flapped inland, their yellow beaks stuffed with sand eels. Flame craned his neck, looking up at all the birds excitedly and almost tripped over his own paws.

Lorna hid a smile. Sometimes it was hard to remember that Flame was a royal prince!

Lunch was delicious. Aunt Marie had even remembered to put in a little packet of dried cat food. Flame munched it happily. Afterwards Ruth, Callum, Lorna and Flame went with Hugh to check out the ledges and cliffs for nesting birds. Lorna put Flame back inside her shoulder bag as they clambered over some extra-big rocks at the base of the cliffs.

As she climbed down the steep rocks on to a stretch of beach, Lorna spotted a brightly coloured dinghy on the shingle. Two boys were sitting nearby, fishing.

'See that dinghy? I *said* it would be OK to row over here,' Callum said pointedly to his dad.

Hugh ignored him and strode over to the boys. 'Hey, you there! Do you

realize this is a nature reserve? I hope
you have fishing permits,' he called.

The boys stood up and turned round.
Lorna recognized them now. It was Sam
and Laurie. Catching sight of Callum,
the older boys waved.

Callum looked sheepish and
pretended not to notice. He kicked at
some sand with one trainer and then
turned his back.

Hugh gave Callum a sharp look and

then turned to Sam and Laurie. 'Hello, lads. What are you up to?'

'Just fishing, Mr Neel,' Sam said politely. 'We usually fish over on the other side of the island. We didn't know we had to have permits for here.'

'Yeah, sorry 'bout that. But we haven't actually caught anything yet,' Laurie said glumly.

'Fish not biting, huh?' Hugh said. His face softened slightly. 'Well, you don't seem to be doing any harm. I'll forget about the permit, just for this once. Make sure you keep away from any nests and young birds and clear up after yourselves, all right? We've had some problems with broken fishing line being left about.'

'Well, it wasn't ours. We always take our rubbish home,' Sam said indignantly.

'Glad to hear it. And take care in that dinghy when you go back, lads. A storm can blow up quickly on that narrow stretch,' Hugh advised as he walked away.

'We will!' Sam and Laurie chorused. 'Thanks, Mr Neel.'

'Just listen to Dad, giving his orders!' Callum muttered, red-faced. 'Why does he have to be *so* embarrassing?' Clenching his fists, he stomped back across the dunes towards their picnic site.

Ruth frowned as she watched her brother go.

Later that afternoon, back from their trip on *Seagull*, Lorna, Flame and Ruth searched for unusual shells. Hugh had gone off to check another area of the reserve, Callum was nowhere in sight, and Lorna's mum, dad, and aunt were at the top of the beach, reading and sunbathing.

'Look at this one!' Lorna exclaimed, bending down to pick up a large pebble. 'It looks just like a kitten curled up asleep!'

'Oh, yes,' Ruth agreed. 'It reminds me of Flame. Look, it's even got amber and white marks on it.'

To her delight, Lorna saw that Ruth was right. She slipped the pebble into her jeans' pocket. After another ten minutes, she pushed a lock of damp red hair off her forehead. 'I'm really hot now. Shall we go for a paddle in this rock pool?' she suggested.

Ruth nodded. 'Great idea!'

Flame sat on a rock as Ruth and
Lorna rolled up their jeans, took off
their trainers and socks, and padded
over to the pool. 'Phew! This stuff's a
bit whiffy,' Lorna said as her foot
squelched on some seaweed.

Ruth wrinkled her nose. 'You're not
kidding!'

Once in the water, they forgot about
the smelly seaweed. They sloshed about,
enjoying themselves. Neither of them
noticed Callum, Sam and Laurie
creeping up on them.

'Got them!' called a triumphant voice.

Lorna whipped round to see Sam
waving their trainers and socks in the
air. 'Very funny. Give them back!' she
demanded.

Sam threw one trainer across to Laurie, who caught it and grinned. 'If you want them back, you'll have to come and get them!'

Lorna put her hands on her hips. She knew just where this was going to end up and it was too hot to chase the boys all over the beach as they threw the shoes and socks to each other. 'Oh, why don't you grow up!' she shouted crossly.

Sam's eyebrows drew together in a scowl. 'I've had just about enough of that snotty kid! I don't care if she is your cousin!' he grumbled to Callum. Lifting his arm, he went to throw the trainers and socks into the pool.

Lorna felt a familiar warm tingling down her back. *Now you've really done it, Sam*, she thought.

She heard a faint crackle of sparks from behind a nearby rock. With a whooshing sound, a sharp breeze lifted all the pongy seaweed into the air. The whole slimy mess shot towards Sam and splatted on to his head and shoulders.

'Argh! Mnnff!' Sam gave a muffled cry. Dropping the trainers, he stumbled about clawing the seaweed off.

'He looks like that shaggy old mop mum uses on the floor!' Ruth said, giggling.

'Look out, Sam!' Callum shouted, but it was too late.

There was a huge splash as Sam toppled into the pool right next to Lorna and Ruth, soaking them both. Moments later, he jumped up furiously spitting out water. Despite being soaked,

Lorna and Ruth fell about laughing and even Laurie and Callum were biting back grins.

'That was a freaky breeze! I've never seen it lift up seaweed like that before,' Ruth said, when she could speak again.

'Mmm,' Lorna agreed. She winked at Flame as he jumped out from behind the rock and stood there twitching his tail. 'That'll teach those mean boys to mess with us!' she whispered to him while everyone was still looking at Sam.

Chapter
SIX

Over the next few days the weather
was dull and rainy, but the big storm
which everyone had been expecting
seemed to have passed by Craggen.

Lorna didn't mind it being gloomy at
first. It was fun exploring the local
market with her cousins. Even
sheltering under an umbrella was OK
with Flame tucked under her arm.

★

Another day, Lorna's parents drove them all to the ferry and they went to the indoor skate park on the mainland.

'This is great, isn't it?' Lorna whispered over her shoulder to Flame as she zoomed back and forth on her rollerblades.

Flame was peering up out of her backpack, his front paws clinging on

tight and his eyes bright with excitement. 'I like it when we go really fast!' he mewed happily.

But by the third day when an angry grey sky hung over the farm and surrounding hills, Lorna found herself longing for sunny weather. 'I'm fed up of shopping and we can't go to the beach. What shall we do?' she asked, glancing at the rain running down the sitting-room window.

Ruth thought hard. 'How about watching TV? Or I could get out my old Barbie dolls?'

'TV or dolls?' Callum said disgustedly, just coming into the room. 'I'd rather eat my own leg! Wait here, you two.'

Lorna smiled to herself. Callum had been great for the last few days away

from Sam and Laurie and now it
looked like he might be having one of
his brainwaves.

Callum reappeared minutes later with
an atlas of the world, a pen and paper
and his dad's stopwatch. Lorna and
Ruth waited, intrigued.

'OK. This game's called Race the
World,' Callum explained, spreading
open the atlas. 'It works like this. We

all make a list of towns from the index. It's fun if you can find really weird-sounding ones. And then we take it in turns to search for them.'

'What's the watch for?' Ruth wanted to know.

'Everyone gets five minutes to find as many towns as they can. That's why it's called a race. Whoever finds the most towns by the end of the game gets this!' He held up a bag of sherbet lemons.

Lorna's mouth watered. 'Sounds great,' she said eagerly. 'Can I have first go at making a list of towns for you two to find?'

'OK,' Ruth and Callum agreed.

Flame folded his front paws beneath him as he watched from the sofa.

It was great fun, finding really

weird-sounding towns and then racing to find them in the atlas. Lorna and her cousins were soon squealing with laughter. An hour passed by, unnoticed. It was Lorna's third go. She was about to turn a page, when suddenly a tiny fluffy shape leapt on to the atlas. 'Watch out, Flame! You're in the middle of the Pacific Ocean!' she said, spluttering with laughter.

As Flame blinked at her with big innocent green eyes and then began washing himself, Ruth started giggling. 'I reckon that's Flame's way of saying that he's bored!'

Callum grinned and reached over to stroke Flame's fluffy fur. 'OK. Have it your way, Flame. Game's over. I vote we share the sweets.'

'Fine by us!' chorused Lorna and
Ruth.

They were all munching sherbet
lemons when the phone rang in the
hall. Lorna heard her uncle pick it up
and start speaking. His voice sounded
serious.

'Uh-oh, sounds like trouble,' said
Ruth to the others.

When Hugh came into the sitting
room a couple of minutes later, he wore
a serious expression. 'That was the local
police. Someone reported seeing smoke
coming from the reserve on Seal Island.
They went to investigate and found
Sam and Laurie. They'd lit a fire and
had been pouring all kinds of stuff on
it to keep it alight.' Hugh shook his
head. 'I can't believe they were so

stupid. And after I let them off about the fishing permit.'

'Sam and Laurie are OK. They were only mucking about,' Callum said. 'It's no big deal.'

'I'm afraid I can't agree with you,' his father replied soberly. 'Who knows what would have happened if it had been a hot day? Fire can easily get out of

control and cause terrible damage to wildlife. Besides, Sam and Laurie could have burned themselves badly. I'm sorry, Callum, those boys are trouble. I want you to stay well away from them.'

'But Da-ad! We were going night fishing tomorrow . . .' Callum burst out and then stopped guiltily as he saw Hugh's set look. 'I was going to tell you about it, honest! I can still go, can't I?'

Lorna couldn't help feeling sorry for her older cousin. It was clear that Uncle Hugh wasn't going to change his mind.

Callum had realized that too. 'You never want me to have any fun, do you!' he shouted tearfully at his father, before storming out. Ruth ran upstairs after her brother, but Lorna heard the bathroom door slam.

'Poor Callum. I hope he's OK,' she said to Flame as she cleared away the remnants of their Race the World game.

Flame nodded sympathetically. 'Perhaps it is best if he stays away from the older boys.'

Lorna remembered how Sam and Laurie had almost run Flame over with the shopping trolley and she had to agree.

That evening, Lorna and Ruth were sitting in Ruth's bedroom listening to some CDs. Lorna was holding the pebble shaped like a curled up kitten and running her fingers over it.

Callum appeared in the open doorway. He glared straight at Lorna. 'You put Dad up to this, didn't you?'

Lorna gaped at him. 'What do you mean?' she asked, puzzled.

'I've been thinking about it. You must have snitched about what happened in the car park. That's why Dad went ballistic at me. It couldn't have been just 'cause of Sam and Laurie lighting fires!'

Ruth rushed to Lorna's defence. 'Stop

it, Callum. Lorna doesn't tell tales; she wouldn't!'

'Huh! And I'm supposed to believe that!' Callum sneered.

Lorna swallowed. She knew that Callum was angry and upset, but he didn't have to take it out on her. 'You can believe what you like! You're just trying to find excuses for your rotten friends. It's Sam and Laurie you want to pick a fight with, not me!' she said furiously.

Callum looked at her closely and seemed to be satisfied. 'Whatever! Anyway, I don't care what anyone says, I *am* going night fishing with Sam and Laurie, so there!' He turned away.

Moments later, Lorna and Ruth heard his bedroom door slam.

'Do you think he meant it about going night fishing?' Ruth asked worriedly.

'No. He's just sounding off. He wouldn't dare, not after what Uncle Hugh said.' But in her heart she wasn't so certain. She'd never seen Callum so upset.

Chapter
SEVEN

The following day, Aunt Marie had to
take some of her woven blankets to a
shop on the mainland. Lorna, Flame
and Ruth went with Marie, while
Lorna's parents went off to shop for
some local treats.

Uncle Hugh was working on the
farm and Callum was helping him. After
delivering the blankets, Aunt Marie

took Lorna, Flame and Ruth to the cinema. 'I think we should leave Flame in the car. He might be scared by the loud noises,' she suggested.

Lorna looked down at Flame, who was curled on her lap in the back seat. She saw him give a slight shake of his head. 'I think he'll be fine, Auntie. I can always bring him back out if he seems upset,' she said.

'All right, love. I'll leave it to you,' Aunt Marie said, smiling.

In the cinema, Flame seemed spellbound by the big screen with its larger-than-life actors and bright colours. The film was an exciting sci-fi adventure. Lorna smiled as Flame twitched his ears and put his head on one side, enjoying the brilliant special effects.

She wondered if he'd been to the cinema before. Perhaps this wasn't the only time he'd visited this world. Lorna felt a flicker of pride that Flame had chosen her for his friend.

After the cinema, they met up again with Lorna's parents. As Aunt Marie drove back across Craggen, dark clouds hung low over the mountains. 'Looks like there's still a chance of us having a storm,' she commented. 'I'd better make sure the animals are all safe tonight.'

When they arrived at the farmhouse, Callum and Uncle Hugh were still out checking on the sheep.

'Can me and Lorna help make supper, Mum?' Ruth asked.

Marie smiled. 'What did you have in mind?'

'Cheese and potato pie?' Lorna suggested. Her mum had shown her how to make it.

'Sounds good. Let's see what I've got to go with it,' her aunt replied.

Lorna and Ruth tied on aprons and got to work. Lorna didn't notice Flame glancing warily over his shoulder before slinking out of the kitchen and running upstairs.

Just as supper was ready, Hugh and Callum appeared.

'Something smells good. I'm starving,' Hugh said.

'Me too,' Callum agreed.

'It's cheese and potato pie, with sausages and beans. Ruth and I cooked it,' Lorna said.

Hugh pulled a face. 'I think I just lost my appetite.'

'Hey!' Lorna said, grinning and digging her uncle in the ribs.

Supper was a great success and Lorna saved a small dishful for Flame, who hadn't appeared for dinner. She felt happy and relaxed. Callum was his funny cheeky self and even told one of his terrible jokes. That evening, they all played Callum's Race the World game. This time they played in teams. Hugh tried to cheat, but he was so bad at it

that everyone noticed. Lorna laughed so
much her ribs ached.

By the time she went up to bed,
Lorna was tired but relaxed. She was
really glad that Callum seemed to have
made things up with his dad and
forgotten all about going night fishing.

She saw the tip of Flame's tail sticking
out from under her pillow. 'You must
be extra sleepy to have missed dinner,'
she teased, slipping her hands beneath it

to pick him up, but he shied away. She frowned. He'd never done that before.

Her face dropped as she realized that the tiny kitten was trembling all over. 'What's wrong? Are you sick?'

Flame flattened his ears and crawled beneath the duvet. 'My enemies are near. If I stay quiet and still they may pass me by,' he told her in a muffled little whine.

Lorna woke up with a start. She sat up staring into the darkness of Ruth's bedroom, wondering what it was that had woken her. She listened carefully and heard a dull thudding sound.

Her first thought was that Flame's enemies had found him. She felt a flicker of alarm for him and her heart missed a beat, but then she felt the kitten's warm little body move close to her. A wave of relief flowed over her. Flame hadn't needed to leave, so he must be safe for now.

'Can you hear that thudding?' she whispered to him.

'Yes. It sounds like a door banging,' Flame mewed softly, jumping off the bed.

Lorna frowned, her heart beating fast. She slipped out of bed after him, crept out of the bedroom, and went slowly downstairs. The farmhouse was creepy in the darkness, but she didn't feel frightened as long as Flame was padding along beside her.

As Lorna went into the kitchen and turned on the light, she saw that the

door to the back porch was open.
As each gust of wind took it, it was
banging back and forth on its
old-fashioned latch.

'That's weird. I know Aunt Marie was
really careful to lock up –' she began,
when suddenly a jagged flash of
lightning lit up the darkened window.
A massive crack of thunder followed
immediately.

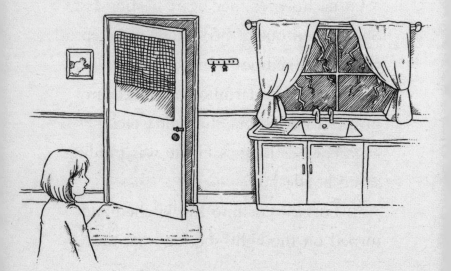

Lorna almost jumped out of her skin. The storm which had been threatening for days was finally here. She listened for any movement from upstairs, but no one stirred, not even when the thunder rolled around for a second and third time. 'They must still be asleep. I expect they're used to storms on Craggen. And Mum and Dad always say that they could sleep through the end of the world!'

Flame's furry brow wrinkled in a frown and his hackles stood up. 'Perhaps someone has tried to get in.'

Lorna thought that wasn't likely. The farmhouse was well hidden in the hills and very hard to find. A dreadful suspicion shot into her mind. 'What about if someone was going *out*, not

trying to get *in*? Come on!' she hissed
to Flame, already racing back upstairs.

'Where are we going?' he mewed
curiously, bounding after her.

'To Callum's room!'

Lorna tiptoed quietly across the hall
and opened Callum's bedroom door.
There was a humped shape in his bed.
It was OK after all then. But as she
drew closer, she could see that the
shape beneath the duvet looked odd.

'Callum?' she whispered, reaching out
to shake him gently, but her fingers
sank right down into the soft duvet.
Throwing it back, she saw the bunched
pillow and rolled clothes.

Lorna gasped. 'He's gone! And I think
I know where – night fishing with Sam
and Laurie. He's going to be in terrible

trouble. We have to go after him, Flame!' As if to underline her words there was another flash of lightning and a crack of thunder.

Lorna quickly pulled her jeans and jumper on over her nightie.

Downstairs, she grabbed a hooded mackintosh and thrust her feet into wellington boots. Scooping Flame up, she slipped him inside the coat and dashed outside.

Rain was lashing down as she splashed across the farmyard and hurried towards the small jetty, where *Seagull* was moored. Another dazzling flash of lightning lit up the narrow sea channel and Lorna gasped with horror.

In that brief glimpse, she had seen a tiny orange shape battling with the wind and the waves. There were three people inside it.

'It's Sam and Laurie's dinghy!' she shouted to Flame above the noise of the storm. 'They're trying to row across to Seal Island. And Callum's with them!'

Chapter
EIGHT

Lorna's first thought was to dash back to the house and wake everyone up, but that would waste precious time.

The thought of that tiny helpless dinghy on the rough sea made her shudder. 'We have to do something – now!' she shouted to Flame above the wind.

Flame nodded. 'Follow me!' He

streaked towards *Seagull*, trailing sparks
like a tiny comet. Lorna didn't hesitate.
She ran after the brave tiny kitten and
quickly got on board. Flame scampered
straight into the cabin. Lorna felt a
familiar warm tingling down her spine
as the biggest silver sparks she'd seen yet
began glowing in Flame's fluffy amber
and white fur.

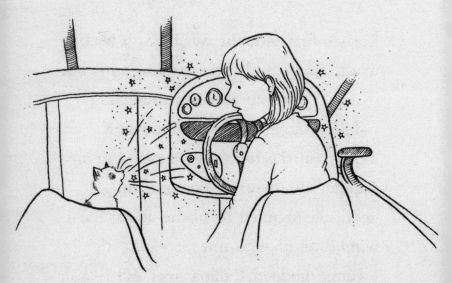

Leaning forward, Flame opened his mouth wide and puffed out a twinkling fountain of bright blue glitter towards *Seagull*'s control panel. For a moment all the controls and the ship's wheel gleamed in the dark and then looked normal again. To Lorna's astonishment the boat's powerful engine rumbled to life and all her lights came on.

'I think it would be best if you drove. Fingers are better at turning a wheel,' Flame purred, holding up his tiny paws.

'Er . . . OK,' Lorna gulped, feeling scared and nervous, but she trusted Flame and knew that he'd never let any harm come to her. 'I'll untie the mooring rope.'

As soon as she came back into the cabin, Lorna took the wheel and *Seagull* seemed to slip away from the jetty all by herself. 'This is easier than I thought,' she said, glancing at Flame who sat peering out at the choppy, white-capped waves.

Thunder roared and lightning flashed, but *Seagull* powered through the sea,

moving ever closer to the tiny dinghy. *Almost there*, Lorna thought. *Hang on Callum, we're coming!*

As the motorboat drew alongside the dinghy, Lorna saw Flame raise a tiny paw and then she felt *Seagull*'s engines slow and the boat came to a full stop, staying put exactly as if she had dropped anchor. Lorna dashed out on to the deck. Holding on firmly to the handrail, she leaned over and looked down through the rain. In the dinghy below her, three scared white faces peered up. She saw that all the boys were wearing lifejackets.

'Dad, I'm sorry . . .' Callum began, looking up at the motorboat. 'Cripes! Lorna what —'

'Never mind that now. Quick! Grab

the ladder and climb up,' Lorna ordered.

For once, the boys didn't argue. Callum and then Sam climbed aboard *Seagull*. Lorna helped them up and then reached down to Laurie. Just as Laurie stepped on to the deck, a big wave crashed against the dinghy and flipped it over. A gust of wind then took it and carried it away until it was just a tiny orange dot against the angry sky.

'We could have been in that,' Sam gasped, horrified.

'Don't think about it. You're safe now. I'm taking you back to shore,' Lorna said. She took the wheel and as the terrified boys gazed out to sea where the dinghy had once been, Flame

magically gunned *Seagull*'s engine into
life. 'We've got them, Flame. And it's all
thanks to you!' she whispered.

'You are welcome,' Flame purred,
settling close by her as the motorboat
swung round and headed back towards
the jetty.

Sam and Laurie huddled together,
shivering under Hugh's spare oilskins.
Callum came and stood next to Lorna

at the wheel. 'I n–never . . . knew you could drive a . . . b–boat,' he stammered, sounding impressed, even though his teeth were chattering.

'Oh, I'm full of surprises,' Lorna said, her eyes gleaming. If only he knew!

'Thank goodness you are, or we'd be in a bigger mess now – or worse. Dad's going to ground me for a year when he hears about this!' Callum said miserably.

'Not if he doesn't find out. Everyone

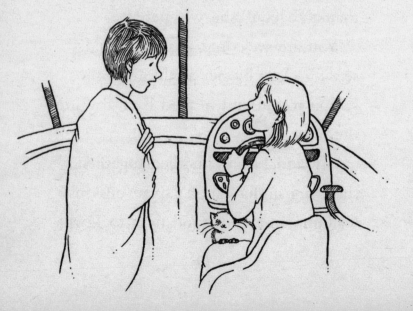

was asleep when I left, despite the storm. I don't think they'd have heard *Seagull*'s engine. If we're lucky, we'll be able to creep back in before they wake up,' Lorna said.

'Really? You're amazing, Lorna!' Callum said, beaming at her.

'She's OK for a girl,' Sam said quietly.

Lorna grinned. That was probably all the thanks she was going to get!

Seagull reached the jetty safely and glided smoothly to a stop at her mooring. As the engine switched off automatically, Lorna jumped out and tied her up.

'Thanks, Lorna!' Sam and Laurie mumbled, before hotfooting it up the jetty and shooting off home.

Callum pulled at her arm impatiently.

'Come on, we'd better hurry. If Mum and Dad wake up and find us gone, we're *both* toast! Flame will follow us.'

'OK, I get the message!' Lorna said. The two of them began jogging towards the back garden as quickly and quietly as they could.

Chapter
NINE

To Lorna's relief there were no lights on at the farmhouse. She, Flame and Callum quickly slipped inside.

'Who . . . who's there?' Ruth's small, scared voice came out of the darkness of the stairwell.

'It's only me and Lorna!' Callum hissed back. 'Hush! You'll wake Mum and Dad.'

'I thought it was burglars!' Ruth whispered, coming down the stairs. 'What are you two creeping about for?'

Callum grabbed his sister's arm and pulled her into the kitchen. 'Come in here and I'll tell you everything!'

Lorna let Callum explain about how she had rescued him, Sam and Laurie

from the dinghy. Ruth listened in amazement, her eyes widening as Callum finished speaking. 'I might have known that Sam and Laurie had something to do with this!' she said crossly. 'You could have all been drowned. You're a complete idiot, Callum! And Lorna's been fantastic, even though you've been so rotten to her.'

'I know you're right,' Callum said, looking subdued. 'Dad tried to warn me, but I was too pig-headed to listen. Tonight's changed all that. Sam and Laurie are history from now on as far as I'm concerned.' He turned to Lorna. 'I'm really sorry I've been such a pain. I'm going to make it up to you, by making this the best holiday we've all

had together. You're a completely
brilliant cousin.'

Lorna blushed hard. 'Thanks. That's
OK.'

Ruth gave a relieved smile. 'Thank
goodness things are back to normal. I
know what we need now.'

'What?' Lorna and Callum chorused
in whispers.

'A group hug!'

'Yuck! Do we have to?' Callum
screwed up his face and made pretend
gagging noises. They all hugged while
trying to muffle their giggles.

After they broke apart, Ruth yawned.
'We'd better go back to bed. Come on,
Callum.' They trudged out of the
kitchen.

'I'll come up in a minute. I'm just

going to get a drink,' Lorna said. She waited until her cousins had gone upstairs before bending down to stroke Flame. 'Thanks again for everything. You've been fantastic tonight,' she whispered.

'I am just happy that I could still be here to help,' Flame purred, rubbing himself against her hand and gazing up at her with bright emerald eyes.

Lorna bent down to pick him up and then laid her cheek against his silky fur. As she breathed in his sweet kitten smell, she felt a big surge of affection for him.

Flame's enemies were still close and they wouldn't stop looking for him. For his own safety, he might have to leave suddenly. And if that happened, Lorna

knew that she was going to have to
be very brave and let her magical
friend go.

Lorna woke suddenly the following
morning. Pinkish dawn light was just
beginning to creep through the
curtains. She stretched out her hand to
stroke Flame, but there was just a tiny
warm dent in the duvet where he had
been lying.

A cold feeling came over her as a suspicion rose in her mind. She quickly got up and padded downstairs.

'Flame! Where are you?' she whispered, checking the hall and kitchen.

Suddenly a bright silver flash came from the sitting room. Lorna rushed inside. A magnificent regal young white lion stood in front of the sofa. She had almost forgotten how impressive and beautiful Flame was as his real self. His white fur glinted with thousands of sparkling points of light.

An older grey lion with a wise kind face stood next to Flame.

And then Lorna knew for certain that Flame's enemies had found him and he was leaving for real this time.

'Prince Flame. We must hurry,' the old grey lion rumbled.

Lorna felt a deep pang of sadness. 'I'll never forget you, Flame!' she said, throwing her arms round Flame's neck.

'You've been a good friend. Be well, Lorna. Stand back now,' Prince Flame said in a deep velvety roar.

As Lorna backed away, there was a final flash, and bright silver sparkles whirled around the two lions like a snowstorm, crackling to the carpet at Lorna's feet. And then the two big cats were gone.

Lorna bit back her tears, glad that Flame was safe. At least she'd had the chance to say goodbye to him. 'Take care, wherever you go,' she whispered.

Her hand brushed against something

in her jeans' pocket. As she reached inside, her fingers closed over something cold.

A slow smile spread over Lorna's face as she took out the pebble shaped like a curled-up kitten. It would always be a wonderful reminder of the marvellous magic kitten who had shared her island adventure.

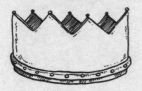
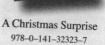

Coming Soon . . .

Magic Kitten

A cute little white and black kitten needs a friend!

Magic Kitten

A Christmas Surprise

SUE BENTLEY

A Christmas Surprise
978–0–141–32323–7

Magic Kitten

A Puzzle of Pa

Flame needs to find a purrfect

And that's how Rosie's worries about moving house get easier to bear when cuddly black kitten Flame becomes part of the furniture . . .

Classro
978–0–1

A Circus Wish
978–0–141–32154–7

A Shimmering Sp
978–0–141–32200–

Coming Soon . . .

Picture Perfect
978–0–141–32348–0

A Splash of Forever
978–0–141–32349–7

puffin.co.uk

More
Magic Kitten
Fun!

Magical Activity Book
978–0–141–32294–0

Sparkling Sticker Book
978–0–141–32293–3

Enter a world of purrfect Magic Kitten fun
with fabulous things to make, do and draw
– and over 100 sparkling stickers!